Published 2020 by Brolly Books
Malvern Victoria 3144 Australia
www.brollybooks.com
Text by Finn Moore | Illustrations by Wendy Straw.
Design by Emma Borghesi.
The Author, Illustrator, and Publisher
have asserted their moral rights in this Work.
ISBN 9781922418074 | 9781922418098 pb

The Girl with No Name

by Finn Moore

illustrated by Wendy Straw

BROLLY BOOKS

Melbourne

The girl with no name lived alone.

She had lived alone for as long as she could remember,

at the centre of a vast forest

that went on for as far as the eye could see.

She was the only one of her kind she had ever met,

and so the need for a name had simply never occurred to her.

This girl lived in a treehouse.

That treehouse was clutched by the very uppermost branches
of the very tallest tree in the forest, and on clear days the girl
with no name would spend hours sitting on the roof.

From such a height, the canopy below sometimes looked

like an ocean of green,

stretching out for miles

in every direction.

The treehouse was very old
and had been built so high in the treetops
that it swayed wildly with each breath of the wind.

The floorboards creaked and complained when walked upon,
and little slivers of starlight wound their way down
through holes in the ceiling at night.

When the rain came, the wood warped and dripped.

The girl with no name
spent most of her time repairing her treehouse
with branches and vines, foraging for food,
and gathering bright stones from the forest floor
to add to her ever-growing collection.

In this way, days passed quietly into years,
time crept slowly by, and the wind and rain bit ever deeper
into the decaying wood of her old, creaking home.

On the day the girl with no name met the raven,

it was cold. And raining.

She was returning home from a day of gathering

more shiny stones for her collection,

intent on taking shelter

from the rising wind and driving rain,

when she saw what looked like

a bundle of black rags

sitting on her windowsill.

Then, the bundle turned its head,

met her stare with two glittering black eyes,

and offered her a hoarse little croak

by way of greeting.

'Hello,' said the girl with no name.

Her voice was almost as hoarse

as the raven's

and whisper-quiet

after a lifetime of

near silence.

'Hello,'

said the raven,

echoing her in its voice of dry leaves rustling over stone.

The bedraggled bird cocked its head to one side,

shifting a little on the sill

and peering down at her with one shining eye.

'Hello.'

The girl and the raven remained where they were for a moment,

looking at each other cautiously.

The raven's glossy black feathers were damp,

and each gust of bitter wind threatened

to dislodge it from its perch.

'You must be cold,' the girl realized.

'Do you want to come inside?'

'Cold,' croaked the raven.

It rapped its beak against the wooden shutter

covering the window, shuffling its clawed feet.

'Cold.'

Quickly, the girl with no name opened the door to her treehouse,

unlatched the shutter from the inside,

and opened the window

to let the bird in.

It hopped down eagerly off the windowsill and onto the table,

flicking rainwater from its wings.

Then, it set about exploring its surroundings,

fluttering from table to shelf to floor,

pecking experimentally

at anything interesting.

The girl with no name wasn't sure what to do next.

She had barely even spoken aloud before that day,

let alone entertained guests.

She offered the raven what little food she had.

This was a mistake, as it turned out, because the bird

made short work of her supply of gathered nuts and berries,

leaving little more than a handful for

tomorrow's breakfast.

Still, she was happy to have shared a meal

with another creature

for the first time.

She produced a towel

and moved to dry the rainwater

from the raven's feathers —

but her first attempt resulted in a stolen towel,

a disapproving caw,

and a thoroughly pecked hand.

The girl retreated

to the other side of the treehouse,

dejected.

After years of silence,

she had finally found someone to talk to,

but now realized she had absolutely no idea what to say.

She attempted conversation,

tried to coax the bird's attention with food and water,

and even attempted to mimic the raven's own melancholy caw,

all in vain.

Her efforts were met with the same silence,

the same intent, black-eyed stare.

Defeated, she sloped back to the other corner of the treehouse

and pulled her collection of stones out from under her bed.

She sat down on the floor and started

sorting through the day's finds,

carefully inspecting, polishing, and organizing

each worthy addition

to the collection.

By the time the second pebble

— a small grey stone

shot through with a vein of glittering quartz —

was in her hand, the raven was already at her side.

It leaned down, pushing the tip of its beak

through a pile of smaller turquoise stones, eyes bright.

'Oh, now you're interested?' said the girl with no name, grinning.
"They're pretty, aren't they? You can find them all over the forest floor.
I like collecting them.'

'Pretty,' croaked the raven. 'Pretty.'

The girl with no name and the raven sat side by side
on the floor, examining each piece of the collection
and rating their worth.

'The raven, for the most part, vacillated between

'pretty' for the ones it approved of,

and a contemptuous caw for the less shiny contenders.

Before long, the storm outside began to ebb, until the hammering

of the rain on the old wooden roof faded to a faint pattering,

then to nothing at all. Still engrossed in her collection,

the girl with no name took no notice.

'Oh, I love this one!' the girl said,

grinning wider than ever as she reached out

to pick up a fist-sized stone.

'It's probably . . .'

But she was interrupted by the sudden sound of

beating wings stirring the air inside the treehouse.

She looked up just in time to see the raven

soar through the still-open window,

leaving nothing but a few black feathers

drifting in its wake.

The girl ran to the window and leaned out.

Already, the raven's silhouette was fading into the distance.

'Don't go!' she tried to call out,

but her voice was still weak from disuse,

and her cry was reduced to a whisper

and snatched away by the wind.

'Don't go,' she said again, quietly.

The girl with no name

had been alone for as long as she could remember,

but now — for the first time — she found that she felt lonely.

In the absence of her new friend,

the once-comfortable silence

of her high, swaying treehouse began to feel bleak.

That evening, she went to bed early,

closing the shutters to block out

the last few rays of light from the still-setting sun.

The girl with no name was awakened the next morning

by what sounded, at first, like the beginnings

of another rainstorm.

There was a faint, insistent tapping sound coming from

outside the treehouse and —

as she dragged herself out of bed and

glumly made her way towards the window —

the sound only grew louder.

With a sigh, the girl opened the shutters,

leaning out to get a better look at the clouds above,

only to be greeted with a pale blue, cloudless sky.

Confused, she looked down . . .

and saw the raven,

sitting on her windowsill once again.

This time, the bird had something in its beak, which it had been —

until recently —

rapping against the shutter like a door-knocker.

Looking very pleased with itself,

the raven flew straight inside without invitation,

and dropped a single, shining pebble down

into her collection.

'Pretty,' the raven croaked,

bobbing its head as though nodding. 'Pretty.'

Then, it turned back to the girl,

who was still standing, stunned,

by the window.

'Hello,'

said the girl with no name,

after only a moment's hesitation.

'Hello,'

said the raven.

It cocked its

head to one

side,

black eyes

sparkling.

'Hello.'